For
Francesca and Pui
Love D

For Laura,
who looks cute
when she wears a cowgirl suit
J. E.

Atheneum Books
for Young Readers
An imprint of Simon & Schuster
Children's Publishing Division
1230 Avenue of the Americas
New York, New York 10020

Text copyright © 2006 by Jonathan Emmett
Illustrations copyright © 2006 by Deborah Allwright
First published in Great Britain in 2006 by
Egmont UK Limited
Published by arrangement with Egmont UK Limited.

The text of this book is set in Nimrod.
Manufactured in Singapore
First U.S. edition 2007
2 4 6 8 10 9 7 5 3 1
CIP data for this book is available
from the Library of Congress.
ISBN-13: 978-1-4169-3652-7
ISBN-10: 1-4169-3652-1

SHE'LL BE COMING 'ROUND THE MOUNTAIN

Jonathan Emmett  **Deborah Allwright**

Atheneum Books for Young Readers
New York London Toronto Sydney

Gather 'round now!
I'm gonna tell y'all about a special visitor. . . .

She'll be coming 'round the mountain
when she comes.

Toot-Toot!

She'll be coming 'round
the mountain when she comes.

Toot-Toot!

Yes, she'll whistle like a train,
as she speeds across the plain.
She'll be coming 'round the mountain
when she comes.

Toot-Toot!

She'll be driving six white horses when she comes.

WHOA BACK!

She'll be driving six white horses when she comes.

WHOA BACK!

They're called Misty, Moonbeam, Milkshake, Stardust, Silvermane, and Snowflake. She'll be driving six white horses when she comes.

WHOA BACK!

Toot-Toot!

She'll be wearing
pink pajamas when she comes.

Tee-Hee!

She'll be wearing pink pajamas
when she comes.

Tee-Hee!

They are flowery and frilly,
and they make her look quite silly.
She'll be wearing pink pajamas when she comes.

Tee-Hee!

WHOA BACK!

Toot-Toot!

She'll be juggling with jelly when she comes.

Squish-Splat!

She'll be juggling with jelly when she comes.

Squish-Splat!

If you ask her as a favor,
she will let you choose the flavor!
She'll be juggling with jelly when she comes.

Squish-Splat!

Tee-Hee!

WHOA BACK!

Toot-Toot!

And she'll dance across the rooftops when she comes.

Yee-Ha!

Yes, she'll dance across the rooftops when she comes.

Yee-Ha!

And you won't believe how nimbly
she can boogie 'round the chimbly.

Yes, she'll dance across the rooftops when she comes.

Yee-Ha!
Squish-Splat!
Tee-Hee!
WHOA BACK!
Toot-Toot!

DINER

JAIL

And she'll paint the whole town purple when she comes.

Bish-Bosh!

Yes, she'll paint the whole town purple when she comes.

Bish-Bosh!

And the place won't
look so glum,
when it's colored
like a plum.

Yes, she'll paint the whole town purple when she comes.

And she'll drink out of a dustbin when she comes.

SLURP-SLURP!

Yes, she'll drink out of a dustbin when she comes.

SLURP-SLURP!

Unless it's ginger ale,
which she drinks out of a pail,

yes, she'll drink out of a dustbin when she comes.

And we'll all go out to meet her when she comes.
"HI, BABE!"

And we'll all go out to meet her when she comes.

"HI, BABE!"

So I hope that you are clear
on what to say when she gets here!

Because she's coming 'round the mountain. . . .

Here she

comes!

"Well, I guess someone must have told y'all that I was comin'!"

Toot-Toot!

Pull on the chain
of a steam whistle

WHOA BACK!

Pull back on the
horse's reins with
both hands

Tee-Hee!

Cover your mouth
with your hands

Squish-Splat!

Juggle the jelly
with both hands

Why don't y'all read the book again,

but this time doing these actions with each of the sounds?